Fischer,
Be your Super self!

Best,
Mike

THE SUPER GUIDE TO BECOMING A SUPERHERO

WRITTEN BY MIKE DELORENZO
ILLUSTRATED BY ALEKSANDRA SZMIDT

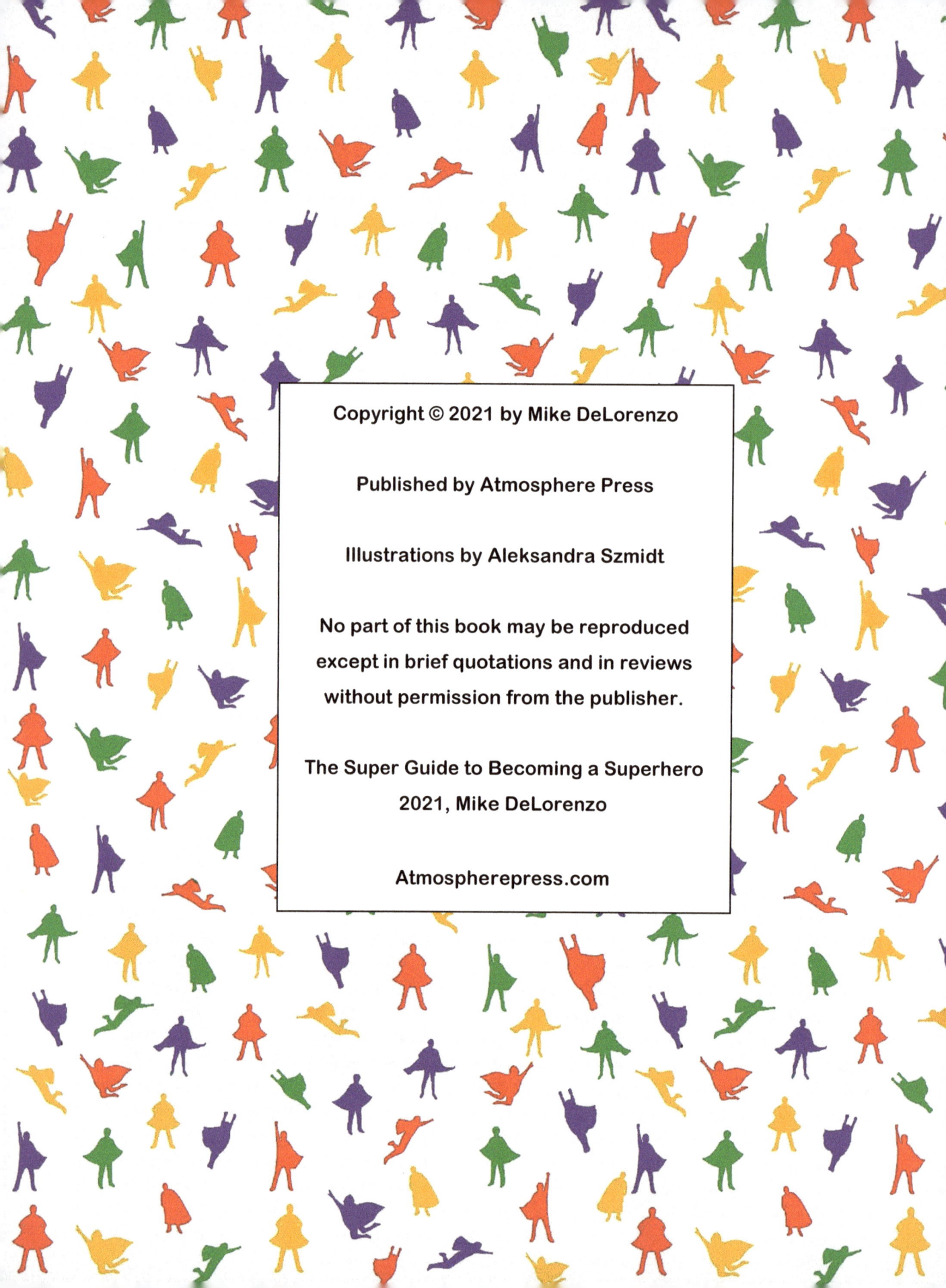

Copyright © 2021 by Mike DeLorenzo

Published by Atmosphere Press

Illustrations by Aleksandra Szmidt

No part of this book may be reproduced except in brief quotations and in reviews without permission from the publisher.

The Super Guide to Becoming a Superhero
2021, Mike DeLorenzo

Atmospherepress.com

To my friends, family, and Hopewell Elementary School community for their unwavering support. A special shoutout to my amazing first grade students for inspiring the creation of The Super Guide to Becoming a Superhero.

You've seen them on TV, you've seen them in movies, you've seen them on billboards, t-shirts, and hoodies. Superheroes are all around us but what makes these superheroes so super?

ARE YOU READY FOR THE TRUTH?

THE REAL TRUTH?

THE UNTOLD TRUTH?

The difference between SUPER people and all the rest is super people always do their best. Doing your best when no one is around sets you apart and that's profound.

Gio has been playing soccer since he was little and has always hoped to play on the school's soccer team. With try-outs in just one week, he squeezed in extra practice each and every day to perfect his shots on goal.

On the day of tryouts Gio scored not one, not two, but three goals during the scrimmage, impressing everyone from his mom to his soon-to-be soccer coach.

While Gio loves spending time on the soccer field, he doesn't like spending time in art class. Nothing is more challenging for Gio than painting. Mixing paints was not so bad, but the actual painting is where Gio ran into trouble.

No matter how hard Gio tried, he just couldn't have his paintings match what he had in his mind. Between a shaky hand and a bushy brush, his painting was no masterpiece at all.

Although it wasn't the prettiest painting in the class, Gio was proud of his work. You might not be a master at everything you try, but you can be filled with great pride knowing you did your best.

Maria enjoys volunteering at the animal rescue in her town. She has always loved playing with the animals and helping take care of them.

Walking the dogs is her favorite part, even though she has to pick up after them. Volunteering to help with the fun and not-so-fun jobs at the animal shelter not only helps the animals stay healthy, it also helps them find new homes.

Maria loves school and especially loves learning new ways to add and subtract. Math is easy for her but challenging for most of her classmates. Maria wanted to help her struggling classmates, but she had never taught math before.

Maria was very nervous about helping her classmates. Despite her fears, she decided that a math study group would be the best way to help.

The study group was a huge success, and the entire class passed their next math test! Anyone can live their life worrying only about themselves, but it takes a super person to help others in need.

For many fourth graders around the world playing the recorder is something to look forward to, but not for Bryce. The right notes never seemed to come out of Bryce's recorder, no matter how hard he blew. Despite how frustrated he was, Bryce never stopped trying.

He practiced in class,

he practiced in the shower,

he even spent time practicing upside down—until one day he finally hit the right note.

Bryce loves making slime! The ooey, gooey, stretchy goodness has always been so much fun to play with but not so much fun to make. Bryce struggled again and again mixing and stirring ingredients but still could not make the perfect slime.

Bryce dumped gobs of glue and boat loads of baking soda into a big bowl, mixed and twisted, but all he was left with was a sticky mess.

While cleaning up, Bryce noticed a can of shaving cream left on the counter and decided to spray some into his bowl.

With a few more twists the mixture was saved, and the super slime he was looking for was born. Although it may not happen at first, you can do anything you put your mind to when you get back up and try once more.

The best superpowers come from within; looking in the mirror is where you begin. Being true to yourself is the most important part, real superpowers come from the heart.

STEP 4: BE YOURSELF!

Grace is a girl with many interests but above all she loves to sing. No one knows what a beautiful voice she has because she only sings quietly when she's alone.

As flyers were posted about the school talent show, Grace was nervous about the thought of standing on stage in front of a packed crowd. Despite her fears, Grace belted out the most beautiful notes that night while sharing her talent with the people around her.

Grace has a great group of friends. Grace's school has a ton of clubs to choose from, everything from the Giant Board Game Club to the Ultimate Frisbee Club. Grace didn't know which to choose and ended up just joining her friends in the Rock Climbing Club.

While racing to the top of the school's rock wall twice a week might sound like fun, Grace was not having much fun at all. Each time Grace made it to the top, she felt anything but happy.

After lots of thinking, Grace decided that the Rock Climbing Club was just not for her, so she joined the school's choir to pursue her passion for singing instead. Recognizing the real you and showcasing what makes you special may just be the most important lesson of all.

The truth about superheroes is that they are no more super than you and I. The truth about supers is they don't need to fly. To be super like the heroes on TV, just follow these steps, that's the key. Don't ever be afraid to be the real you, there's always room for one more in our superhero crew!

About the Author

Mike DeLorenzo is an elementary school teacher from New Jersey whose passion for picture books was ignited after beginning his teaching career in the fall of 2020. While teaching through a global pandemic he became inspired by his students' love of picture books to begin drafting his own. Within months this led to the creation of his first picture book, *The Super Guide to Becoming a Superhero*. In addition to his passion for education, Mike enjoys going on outdoor adventures and spending time with family and friends.

About the Illustrator

Aleksandra Szmidt is an award-winning children's book illustrator who grew up in the south of Poland before journeying to the other side of the world to live in New Zealand. Adept in both digital and traditional techniques, Aleksandra works from her home studio, creating one-of-a-kind artworks for clients across the globe. Her love of drawing children, animals and landscapes takes her back to the fun and adventures of her own childhood. To this she loves to add layers of magic and humour that are more imagination than reality. Aleksandra's work brings her immense joy and a deep emotional connection to her art.

About Atmosphere Press

Atmosphere Press is an independent, full-service publisher for excellent books in all genres and for all audiences. Learn more about what we do at atmospherepress.com.

We encourage you to check out some of Atmosphere's latest releases, which are available at Amazon.com and via order from your local bookstore:

Do Lions Cry?, by Erina White

Sadie and Charley Finding Their Way, by Bonnie Griesemer

Silly Sam and the Invisible Jinni, by Shayla Emran Bajalia

Feeling My Feelings, by Shilpi Mahajan

Zombie Mombie Saves the Day, by Kelly Lucero

The Fable King, by Sarah Philpot

Blue Goggles for Lizzy, by Amanda Cumbey

Neville and the Adventure to Cricket Creek, by Juliana Houston

Peculiar Pets: A Collection of Exotic and Quixotic Animal Poems, by Kerry Cramer

Carlito the Bat Learns to Trick-or-Treat, by Michele Lizet Flores

Zoo Dance Party, by Joshua Mutters

Beau Wants to Know, a picture book by Brian Sullivan

The King's Drapes, a picture book by Jocelyn Tambascio

You are the Moon, a picture book by Shana Rachel Diot

Onionhead, a picture book by Gary Ziskovsky

Odo and the Stranger, a picture book by Mark Johnson

Jack and the Lean Stalk, a picture book by Raven Howell

Brave Little Donkey, a picture book by Rachel L. Pieper

Buried Treasure: A Cool Kids Adventure, a picture book by Anne Krebbs

CPSIA information can be obtained
at www.ICGtesting.com
Printed in the USA
LVHW071029030821
694405LV00002B/17